ALSO BY STEPHEN HUNECK

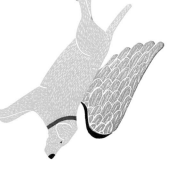

Sally Goes to Heaven

Written and Illustrated by
Stephen Huneck

Abrams Books for Young Readers
New York

Artist's Note

To create a woodcut print, I first draw the design of the future print in crayon, laying out the prospective shapes and colors. I then carve one block of wood for each color in the appropriate shape. The result is a series of carved blocks, one for each color in the print. After a block has been inked with its respective color, acid-free archival paper is laid onto the block and hand rubbed. I repeat the process for each color block. When this process is completed, I then hang the prints to dry. —S.H.

Library of Congress Cataloging-in-Publication Data

Huneck, Stephen.
Sally goes to Heaven / Stephen Huneck.
pages cm
Summary: A beloved dog dies and goes to heaven, where she
lives happily and helps find her family on earth a new pet.
ISBN 978-1-4197-0969-2
[1. Dogs—Fiction. 2. Pets—Fiction. 3. Death—Fiction.
4. Heaven—Fiction.] I. Title.
PZ7.H8995Sajm 2014
[E]—dc23
2013010063

Text and illustrations copyright © 2014 Stephen Huneck Gallery, Inc.
Book design by Robyn Ng

Printed and bound in China
10 9 8 7 6 5 4 3 2 1

Abrams Books for Young Readers are available at special discounts when purchased in quantity for premiums and promotions as well as fundraising or educational use. Special editions can also be created to specification. For details, contact specialsales@abramsbooks.com or the address below.

ABRAMS
THE ART OF BOOKS SINCE 1949

115 West 18th Street
New York, NY 10011
www.abramsbooks.com

This book is in memory of Stephen and Gwen Huneck and is dedicated to their Dog Chapel on Dog Mountain.

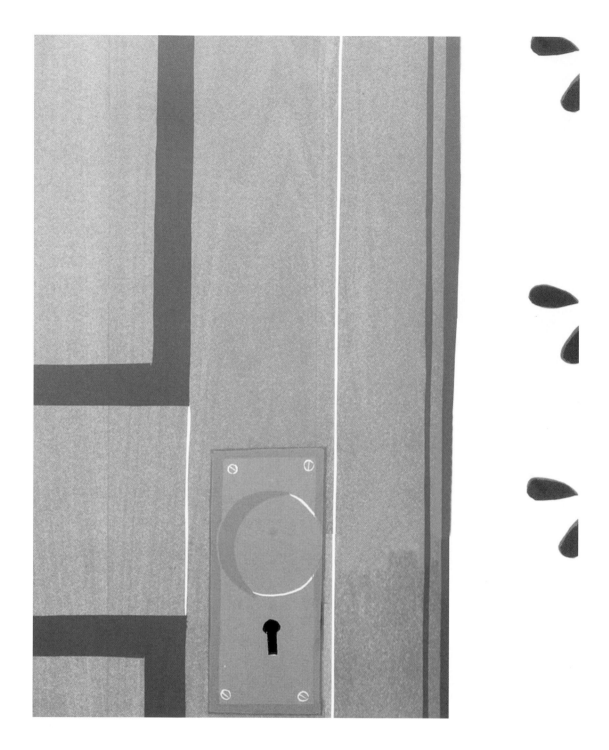

Sally wakes up when she hears
the front door close.

She rises slowly from her bed, careful
not to strain her aching joints.

She walks slowly over to her food dish
to have breakfast. After a bite or two,
Sally realizes she is not hungry.

Sally spends the rest of the day
lying in the sun.

The next morning, Sally wakes up in heaven.

The first thing she notices is that her aches
are gone. She runs in circles really fast.
No pain at all! She's never felt so good.

Sally wishes she could comfort her family and friends and let them know that her pain is gone.

But Sally isn't sad for long.
She knows that someday they will
all be together again in heaven.

Sally decides to go exploring. She sees a giant mound. She approaches it cautiously, sniffing all the way. The closer she gets, the better she smells it. And the better it smells!

The mound is a gigantic pile
of dirty socks! Hurray!

Exploring some more, Sally discovers there aren't any fences and no one is tied up. They are free to do whatever they want.

Also missing are animal shelters.
Every dog has a home.

There are dogs playing, running, and chasing one another everywhere Sally looks.

In heaven, all animals play together as friends.

When they see Sally, the rabbits don't
run away. And the birds don't fly away.
Even the cats join in the games.

The grass is as soft as a carpet.

Sally can pounce and bounce
on the rubbery sidewalk.

Sally thinks of her favorite treats and soon discovers an ice cream stand on every block.

She learns that meatballs grow on bushes, and even the smallest dogs can reach them.

In heaven, Frisbees fill the sky!

Someone is always ready to
throw a ball or toss a stick.

And there are pools
and ponds and oceans
to swim and play in.

Sally thinks the only thing better than all that she sees would be a tummy rub.

When she lies on her back, a line of children wait their turn to rub Sally's tummy!

There are so many new
friends to meet and
dogs to greet. This
could take forever!

Growing sleepy, Sally discovers a long, long couch that stretches as far as she can see. Curled up on it is every kind of dog and cat imaginable.

Sally snuggles up against a pillow, but before she takes a nap, she makes a wish. She wishes very hard that her family will adopt another dog soon.

A dog who will love them and take care of them just like Sally did. And you know what?

Sally's wish was heard and granted.
But that is a whole new story.

Shhhh. Sally is dreaming. There is so
much more for her to explore and see.